The Timid Rabbit

Words and pictures:
Elizabeth Shaw

THE O'BRIEN PRESS
DUBLIN

First published 2007 by The O'Brien Press Ltd,
12 Terenure Road East, Rathgar, Dublin 6, Ireland
Tel: +353 1 4923333; Fax: +353 1 4922777
E-mail: books@obrien.ie
Website: www.obrien.ie

Text: originally written in German by Elizabeth Shaw; © Der
KinderbuchVerlag in der Verlagsgruppe Beltz, Weinheim, Basel, Berlin.
Translated into English by the author and rewritten by Íde ní Laoghaire;
copyright © the Elizabeth Shaw estate and The O'Brien Press.

Illustrations copyright © the Elizabeth Shaw estate

Copyright for layout, editing, design
The O'Brien Press Ltd

ISBN 978-1-84717-062-0

British Library Cataloguing-in-Publication Data
A catalogue reference for this title is available
from the British Library

1 2 3 4 5 6 7 8 9 10
07 08 09 10 11 12

The O'Brien Press receives

Can YOU spot the
panda cub
hidden in the story?

Timmy was a
timid rabbit.

He was **afraid**
of **everything**.

He lived with his
dear old granny.

She was very **timid** too.

'Do be **careful**,
little one,' said Granny.
'Something **bad**
could happen to you!'

Timmy was afraid
of **dogs**.

Granny said,
'**Dogs bite!**'

He was afraid
of the **dark**.

Granny said,
'There are **ghosts**
and **robbers**!'

He was afraid of **water**.

Granny said,
'You could **drown**
in the water!'

He was afraid
of **big boys**.

Granny said,
'They could **hurt** you!'

'Cowardy, cowardy custard!' shouted the children.

Timid Timmy,

they called him.
They did not want
to play with him.

Timmy wept.
He was very unhappy.

'You must stop
being afraid,'
said kind Uncle Henry.
'Just **don't be scared**
any more!'

That was easy to say.
But poor Timmy
was still scared.

Timmy played
with baby Olly instead.

One dark day
the fox
sneaked into the village.

The rabbits were
terrified!

They ran away
as fast as they could.

They hid in their houses.

Timmy and baby Olly
ran away too.

But little Olly
could **not** run fast.

And the wicked fox
caught little Olly.

'The wicked fox is going **to eat** little Olly!'
cried Timmy.
'What will I do?'

Timmy **forgot**
to be afraid.
He caught the fox
by the tail.

The fox dropped
little Olly.

The fox bared his teeth.
He was very angry.

'I'll drag that rabbit
into the thistles!'
said the fox.

But Timmy did not let go.

The fox raced
across the field.

But Timmy
still held on to his tail.

The fox ran
towards a tree.

Timmy made a plan.

He let go!

The fox ran
into the tree!

He was covered
in bumps and bruises.

The fox **ran away**
as fast as he could.

Timid Timmy
and little Olly
were very pleased.

The other rabbits
were very pleased too.

The mayor of the town
gave Timmy a medal.

'Just look at that!'
said Uncle Henry.
'What a **brave** rabbit!'

All the rabbits shouted,
'Hurray!'

But Granny sighed.
'Oh dear! Terrible things
might have happened
to you,' she said.

'Well, I didn't have **time** to think of that, Granny,' said Timmy.

'I had to think of **little Olly**!'

Next day
all the children
called out:
'Here comes
**Timmy,
the Brave Rabbit**!'

And they all went off
to play together.

And Timmy
was **not** timid
any more.